AUTUMN
PUBLISHING

Published in 2022
Published in the UK by Autumn Publishing
An imprint of Igloo Books Ltd
Cottage Farm, NN6 0BJ, UK
Owned by Bonnier Books
Sveavägen 56, Stockholm, Sweden
www.igloobooks.com

0322 002
2 4 6 8 10 9 7 5 3
ISBN 978-1-80108-110-8

Printed and manufactured in China

Disney
My First Stories

WHO'S NOT SLEEPY?

Chip had a very busy day. Now it's **time for bed**.

"But I'm not sleepy, Mama," he says.

Mrs Potts insists. "**Goodnight**, Chip. I'll see you in the morning, love."

Chip hops up and heads for the dining room.

"What are you doing?" he asks Belle and the Beast.

"Eating dinner," says Belle.
"Shouldn't you be in bed?"
"I'm not sleepy," says Chip.
"Maybe a little snack would help."

Chip sees his mother's tea cart across the room.

He jumps up to play with some spoons and napkins.

Just then, Lumiere comes by. "Still up?" he asks.

"I'm not sleepy," replies Chip.

"Follow me," says Lumiere. "I'll light the way to bed."

When Chip gets to the cupboard,
Lumiere turns to walk out of the room.

His light casts a big shadow on the wall.
Chip gets scared and starts to cry.

Cogsworth hears Chip crying and rushes in.

"Now, now," he says. "Don't be scared. I know something that will make you laugh! Here, Footstool! Come on, boy!"

It works! Footstool wags his tassles and Chip giggles.

"Do you think you can fall asleep
now?" asks Cogsworth.
"No," says Chip. "I'm still not sleepy."

"I suppose one short ride couldn't hurt," says the clock.

Off they go down the long hallway.

Suddenly, they bump into the tea cart!

"Oh, dear," mutters Cogsworth. "There go the dishes!"

Fifi the feather duster hurries over. "Don't worry," she says.

"Since I'm not sleepy," says Chip, "I'll help you clean up."

"All done," says Fifi, putting the last dish away. "Now off to bed!"

"But I'm still not sleepy," says Chip.

"Perhaps Belle will read to you, chérie," Fifi says.

Belle reads two stories while Chip and the Beast listen.

"You must be sleepy now," says Belle.

"Nope!" Chip says. "Not yet."

"I have an idea," says the Beast. "Come with me."

He takes the little teacup outside on the balcony.

Belle soon follows them.

"Did you ever see so many stars?" the Beast asks.

"Why don't you make
a wish?" says Belle.
"Okay," Chip says. "Maybe that
will work."

He picks a star and makes a wish. "Nope," Chip says. "I'm still not sleepy."

Back inside, Mrs Potts tries singing Chip a lullaby.

"Thanks, Mama," says Chip. "But I'm still not sleepy."

"Oh, dear," says Mrs Potts. "I'm all out of ideas!"

"What about a goodnight kiss?" asks Chip.

Mrs Potts walks Chip back to the cupboard.

She kisses him goodnight. "See you in the morning, love."

"Now I'm sleepy," Chip says with a yawn. "**Goodnight**, Mama! **Goodnight**, my friends. Sweet dreams, everyone!"